Once upon a time in China, there was a great and noble teacher called Master Ming. Although there were many teachers in the country, none were as widely respected as Master Ming.

In his youth, Ming was known as one of the most handsome warriors in the land. He had long black hair, fine features and intense dark eyes. His body was like a finely tuned weapon, honed for fighting. He was a fierce opponent in hand to hand combat and had many scars on his face and body to show how aggressively he fought. In fact, he was often presented to the emperor as a warrior worthy of commendation. He spoke harshly of the men he defeated, calling them weak and undisciplined.

On one such occasion, the emperor brought a defeated prisoner forward. Ming looked at the defeated warrior, spat in his face and kicked him. The emperor looked at the prisoner and then looked at Ming. He called Ming forward and told the guards to give Ming to the enemies. Ming froze and then knelt to the ground bowing before the emperor. "I did not intend to displease you, my emperor. Please tell me what you would have me do to redeem myself."

The emperor looked at Ming and told him to stand. "I do not do this as punishment Ming. I do this to create in you the wholeness and compassion that you are lacking. I know you will survive physically. And when you return, I know that you will be worthy of my commendations."

When Ming did return to his home one year later, he had not acquired any more battle scars but had a serenity and calmness that became a hallmark of his demeanour. He was brought to the emperor. Ming bowed with reverence.

"Tell me about your year with the enemy," said the emperor. "My emperor," answered Ming. "Your decision to send me to the enemy's land was a good one. I am ashamed to think of what I was and what I would have become." "Tell me more," invited the emperor.

"These people did not want to fight us. In fact, when I first came to their village, it was I who was abusive. I shouted at them, calling them cowards. They didn't fight back. I thought they were weak.

Even though I treated them with such disrespect, they invited me into their homes, they welcomed me as a neighbour and they showed me their customs. They included me in their family gatherings. I witnessed how they resolved disputes and how they treated their least able villager with utmost compassion and care. I was amazed at how they allowed themselves such open hearts. They did not have a need to guard their affections, only their negative opinions. Those they expressed only after much consideration. My quick tongue and quick temper was a curiosity to the villagers. I soon became a source of amusement.

After a few months I decided to watch what they did. Yes they had problems too, but they approached them with diplomacy and conciliation. They used humour, understanding and creativity as the corner-stones of their mediation.

One of their mediators was a woman! I have never seen a woman given such a prestigious role. I couldn't believe it, but she was fair and just in her deliberations. The funniest time was when she mediated a dispute between two men both claiming the same woman as their future wife. She decided the woman should ask each man to do one thing. The woman decided that they should entertain the village and that the villagers should choose the best one.

One of the men not only dressed up as a woman but served food to all the villagers. The villagers saw that his humour and humility would be good qualities in a marriage. The other man talked loudly and boastfully but did not impress the villagers. The woman married the first man and had their first child just before I left."

The emperor smiled. "Welcome back Ming. You have learned well." Ming bowed again and started to leave. "You will not be going back to the battlefield Ming," the emperor continued. "Instead, you will be my personal advisor." Ming was shocked. "Of course my emperor. It would be my great honour." "I have a garden estate for you to stay. It will be a retreat for wise and just council." Then the emperor got up and left the room.

It was in this capacity as the emperor's advisor that he became known as Master Ming. He had quiet, gentle power. He had wisdom steeped in experience. Many who knew him agreed that he had the gifts of peace and love. His power was not a formal authority but a power based on insight and compassion.

It was so well known that the great rulers continued to come to him for advice and counsel even after their disputes were resolved. His guidance was helpful and clear. He could see and understand what approach or remedy was needed in any given situation. His gift for bringing peace and love was a much needed resource in a world filled with war and armament. But even the armed factions desired to put down their weapons and find peace with each other. He approached all people with grace, respect and humility. He came to be known as the gentle Master.

Although he was greatly revered, there were still many sceptics who came wanting to prove that they were more powerful than him. While expertly trained in several martial arts, he would never agree to fight nor would he be pushed over like a rag. He consistently spoke with eloquence, gentleness and understanding. As a result of Master Ming's calm inner strength, leaders who came to see him in an angry and hostile state always left with forgiveness in their heart.

Due to his humble gifts, Master Ming was sought out by many people yearning to study under his tutelage. He did not allow many into his sanctuary but every year he selected five students to join him in community and learn the lessons he had to teach.

This year he chose Lang, Shin, Quiang, Tai, and Lan. It was the first year that he allowed a young girl to study with him. There was great controversy about this selection as girls were not seen to be worthy of such important teaching. Lan's parents were also confused. Women did not assume positions of high rank. They might be wives of high ranking officials but never themselves officials. Their place was to support men and to work in the background. To be summoned as a student of Master Ming was unheard of. But Master Ming was adamant that he wanted Lan. "She has a special gift," he said, but did not elaborate. If she did not come, the spot would remain vacant for the year.

Lan's parents were secretly pleased and relieved that Lan had this opportunity. Lan was an unusual girl and lived in her own world of imagination. They worried about her. She did not learn her social graces easily and spent much time in a dreamlike state, always treating her dream world equally to the real world. They worried that the other villagers would think that she was cursed and that they might ostracize the entire family. So they did their best to shelter and protect her from their neighbours' judgments by keeping her in the house as much as they could.

Lan was a pretty girl with delicate features and eyes full of wonder. She loved art and singing and would often sing and paint in their attic. Her hands were slender and moved gracefully when she painted. Her voice was full of emotion expressing sentiments and sensitivities beyond her years. Lan's parents knew they would never be able to provide the life that Lan needed, a life beyond serving men.

On the day that the new students arrived, Master Ming only saw the four young men at the door.

"Where is Lan?" he asked.

"She's over there," young Quiang said. "She's talking to that tree," he said as the other students giggled.

"Oh, she's found it already," Master Ming whispered. He ignored the four men and walked toward Lan. He walked slowly and quietly and stopped a short distance away from the young girl. She had her hands on the tree and she was looking up at the leaves, speaking quietly and gently, as though quieting a horse.

When she was finished, she turned to Master Ming and said without shyness, "I know this tree. It's as though I've known it my whole life. I didn't realize how beautiful it was. See how it shimmers in the light? Some of the seeds have already blown away but there are still plenty left."

Master Ming smiled. "Welcome Lan. I'm glad you found your tree. It is beautiful. I've been taking care of it for many years."

Lan smiled as she spoke. "It's grown strong under your care Master."

Lang, Shin, Quiang and Tai slowly walked up behind Master Ming and were all stunned that Lan was talking to the great Master in such a familiar tone. This was totally unfitting for a student/Master conversation. One was always to hold a Master with reverence and awe, never to speak unless spoken to. This girl knew nothing of etiquette. Nor did she know her place. A spirit of jealousy was beginning to brew amongst them.

"Lang, what do you see in front of you?" asked Master Ming, pointing to the tree.

"It's a tree Master," Lang said tentatively.

"Do you see anything unusual about it?" Master Ming continued.

"I see brown leaves. Most of them have fallen off and the trunk has some holes in it where birds have pecked. It looks like an ordinary tree Master."

"Shin, do you see the same as Lang or something different?" the Master asked Shin.

"I see the same as Lang, Master."

Master Ming asked Quiang and Tai the same question and they both answered that it was an ordinary tree. Sharing a feeling of dissatisfaction, all four young men felt that the Master was after more, that somehow their observations were not the response he was looking for.

"Lan, what do you see?" Master asked.

"Master, this is a very special tree. The leaves are not leaves at all. In fact they are seeds which shine in the sun. When they are ripe, the wind will take them far away, to grow in other fields, other lands. It's not ordinary at all."

The young men looked puzzled. It was just an ordinary tree with most of its leaves gone. How could Lan have such a different vision before her? They looked at each other thinking, "She must be one of the witches our parents always talked about." No one ever saw one of these witches but there were stories that these witches were dangerous and they saw strange visions and heard evil voices. Of course, Lan didn't look dangerous at all. She was just a young girl of fourteen. But there was no doubt that she saw things that weren't there and she was talking to the tree.

"Why can they not see this tree Master?" Lan asked softly.

"Because it is your tree Lan. And you are right. You have known it your whole life. The others cannot see it because they are not ready to see it." The men were puzzled. How could they not be ready to see it? It was as plain as the rice fields they came from. It was a tree like

all the others in the area. Not wanting to be disrespect-
ful but curious about what the Master meant, Quiang
ventured a question. "Why are we not ready to see it
Master? And when may we be ready to see this beautiful tree?"

"That depends entirely on you Quiang." And with
that, Master Ming retired to his study for the rest of
the day.

Master Ming did not come out to meet the students
for another month. During the first week, the students
got to know the grounds and the buildings. They met all
of Master Ming's helpers.

By the second week, Shin and Quiang got into a
routine of helping out with the work and spending a few
hours in meditation. Lang and Tai did not have a routine
and as the second week drew to a close, they became

bored. They spent the majority of their time together walking the grounds. When they passed Lan's tree, they would always comment. "If she came from my village, the carpenter would probably have cut down that tree to make a table!" Lang laughed.

"If that tree were in my village, it would probably be cut down for firewood!" Tai said and they both laughed harder. "What is it about that girl? Why did the Master treat her like she was so special?"

Lan spent her time doing what she loved: singing and painting. Sometimes, after spending hours painting, she became tired and slept under her tree. She heard what Lang and Tai said about her tree when they passed by as she was lying in the tall grass unnoticed. "Why can't they see this tree?" she wondered to herself. "And if they couldn't see it, could anyone besides Master Ming and me see it?"

Sometimes, if Lang and Tai saw her by the tree, they would say, "How are you Lan? And how is your beautiful tree? Has it said anything to you today?" And they would continue walking, laughing to themselves. By the time the fourth week came and went, Lan was starting to wonder herself whether seeing this beautiful tree was worth the ridicule.

When Master Ming met the students again, he was somehow different. He was not as gentle and warm as he was the first day. "Lang, Shin, Quiang, Tai and Lan," said Master Ming sternly. "You have been here for a month now. What have you to show for it?" The students looked down.

Shin was the first to speak. "Master, I have repaired the wood shed and I have spent four hours a day in meditation." Master Ming looked at Shin for a few moments before casting his eye on the next student.

"I have assisted your helpers to prepare all the meals and do the laundry and I too have spent four hours a day in meditation," said Quiang with quiet confidence.

Master Ming turned to Lang. "And what have you been doing Lang?"

Lang said just as boldly, "I have been walking these beautiful grounds and getting to know all of the plants and animals."

"And you Tai. What have you been doing?"

"I have also been enjoying these beautiful grounds. There are many beautiful plants and trees."

"And Lan. What have you been doing?"

Lan, now timid after enduring a month of teasing from the others, said, "I have been enjoying the garden too Master…and I've been singing and painting."

Master Ming looked a few moments longer at Lan. "You have all had enough time to get acquainted with the land. You will now become more acquainted with the ways of Mother Nature. Starting tonight, you will live outdoors. There are no predatory animals so you are safe. But there is no better teacher than the great earth herself. Try to get to know her. Get to know her rhythms and her rules. She makes no exceptions. I have instructed the helpers that they are not to talk to you or feed you. Mother Nature will provide. I will see you again when I sense that you are ready."

"What are we supposed to be learning?" Lang said to the others when Master Ming had left.

"I could have stayed outside in my own village," said Tai. "I thought he was supposed to be teaching us, not just leaving us by ourselves to learn whatever we want."

"Perhaps he is teaching us," Quiang offered. "After all, he is the Master. He must know something that we don't."

Lan was silent. She did not want to bring attention to herself.

"Well, little girl, at least you can spend more time with your tree," Lang said curtly in Lan's direction.

Lan was scared. She had never been on her own outside before. She was too afraid to ask the other young men for help. And besides, they were much older than her, probably at least ten years. She walked over to her tree, now not even as beautiful as it was when she first arrived. It looked older and it didn't shimmer like it did before. The ripening seeds were looking an awful lot like regular leaves and they were drying up and falling off. "Oh no, even my tree is leaving me and becoming like all the others!" Lan whispered.

She slept very close to the tree that night, hoping that she was wrong, and desperately wishing that it would look beautiful again in the morning. But morning came and the tree looked nothing like it did on the first day. It looked just like all the other trees. If she hadn't been sleeping under it, she would not have been able to tell which one it was.

Lan was discouraged but she didn't lose hope. She sang her songs and made pictures in the sand with pieces of branches. She slept under her tree. After a

whole day, she became so hungry, she had to lie down. She hadn't given any thought to what she would do for food. Where were the other men? What were they doing? Just as she began to wonder about the others, she heard laughing. The four students were coming toward her.

"There you are little sister. Come. We have been wandering around these surrounding woods and there is a lake close by. We caught some fish for dinner tonight and there is one for you. Shin has gathered some berries and we will be fed tonight. Now, you see, we aren't all bad, are we? Come now. Forgive us for our teasing. We need to work together now. You can help us to cook the dinner and during the day, we will gather food for the next night."

Lan was relieved. She had been very worried about how she was going to survive. She needed the help of the young men and she was glad they found her because she would have been lost trying to find them. "Thank you," she said quietly.

"There now, we are all friends, right Lang?" said Quiang.

"That's right. Even little sister here." For the first time in many days, they all ate together and fell asleep quite content.

The five students were beginning to form a small community. They developed a routine and helped each other. They each had their separate work. Some fished while others hunted small animals. Some gathered the plentiful plants, berries, fruit or vegetables. Others contributed by collected firewood for the evening fire.

After a number of weeks though, the weather was starting to get colder. Tai made the suggestion that they start building a small cabin.

"We don't know how long we will be living out here and it will take a lot of work just making a temporary shelter. If we want a cabin, we will need sharp tools to cut down larger branches."

The five agreed and they spent some of their time every day putting up a temporary shelter and gathering and making sharper tools.

Lan was feeling much stronger and saw her place in this small community of five students. She forgot all about her special tree. After all, wasn't the point of this teaching to try and live in harmony with Mother Nature? She was supposed to learn how to work together with other people and to contribute her skills and effort for

the good of all. Lan felt sure that she was learning what Master Ming intended.

Lang was the natural leader of the group. Whenever he spoke, it was with assurance. He helped the other students when they were unsure of the right step. He pitched in when strength was needed and he coordinated efforts when there was a big job at hand.

Tai was Lang's first man. He was there to lend support to Lang's decisions. He explained to the rest of the group why Lang's ideas made sense. He was the first to get started on any of Lang's projects.

Quiang was equally as strong as Lang in his self-assurance but he did not offer his ideas boldly. He was quiet and reserved and he was not quick to act on Lang's decisions although he never challenged any of his comrade's decisions openly. He would often wait until the others started and then approach Lang for a quiet talk. They would frequently walk through the woods talking.

Lan never heard the conversations and she never asked what they were about. She was content to work in the areas that were of help to the group. Decisions could be left to the men. This must be what her parents had been trying to teach her; to understand her role and fit into society. As Lan became more familiar with the tasks and how she was contributing, she felt a certain comfort and contentment in fulfilling them.

The cold temperatures were no longer tolerable at night and it was finally time to start building the winter cabin. The men had been working on the tools necessary to cut the trees. Lan gathered enough moss, leaves and branches to attach to the roof and to the outside of the walls to keep the wind out. She was pleased with her progress.

Lang, Tai and Quiang spent much of their days in other areas of the garden, working to gather larger pieces of wood and hunting for the day's meal. Shin and Lan were left to help with the local gathering and preparation of the shelter and food.

Many hours were spent in silence as Lan and Shin attended to their activities. It was during these times of silence that Shin took note of the way that Lan worked, quickly, accurately and happily. Lan felt more and more at ease with Shin. He had always been the quietest of the four men and working with him for days on end only helped her to feel more comfortable with his presence. He had a calm and accepting approach with her. He never chastised her and accepted her occasional singing with patience. And he was always mindful of his words and his work. Shin encouraged her and appreciated her efforts.

One day, after the evening meal, Shin asked Lan, "How did Master Ming come to choose you as his student?"

"My parents kept me inside the house or hidden for most of my life," Lan started. "They meant well but they were ashamed of me." She became suddenly sad as she remembered this. "Why would they be ashamed of you? You are a beautiful girl," Shin said.

"My parents were afraid that people would say that I was a witch. I never really understood what that meant until they told me the story of the grocer's wife in the next village. The story went that she had given birth to a

baby who died at birth. After that, she started acting as though her dead baby was still alive.

She would start to talk to the baby and talk to others as though the baby were in her arms even though it wasn't. Her husband tried to stop her, making excuses for her to their neighbours but it didn't help. After a few weeks, the neighbours started calling her a witch, saying that she was talking to the dead and that the ancestors would curse the whole village and bring evil spirits to haunt them. They wanted them both to leave immediately. But the husband thought this was just talk and didn't do anything. The villagers got more and more hostile. The husband tried to get them to understand that she didn't mean to hurt anyone. The neighbours were so fearful of the prospect of being cursed that they broke into their house, dragged the woman out and drowned her in the lake."

Lan stopped. "My parents were afraid the same thing would happen to me. I knew I wasn't a witch but I understood why they were afraid. I used to hear the trees talking and see such beautiful things that they couldn't see. They weren't frightening voices. In fact, they were like my friends. It wasn't all the trees, just some of them. Others just stood like silent partners, letting the more vocal trees speak for them but supporting all they expressed. I didn't see many people outside my family but my parents let me walk in the woods by myself when no one was around.

The woods became my friends, but I never lived out there. I never had to find my own food or shelter. My life was mostly inside our house. My parents felt guilty about keeping me inside so they brought me things to keep me amused. I loved to sing and paint mostly and spent most of my life doing this. But there was one tree that I kept hearing and seeing all those years. It wasn't one that spoke to me in the woods. It was something that spoke to me in my heart and in my mind. It came to me in my dreams. It was a most beautiful tree. A tree that sparkled in the sun and had seeds that blew in the wind. I told my parents about this dream all the time. They listened patiently but they always told me that it wasn't real; that it was just a dream. I think they thought most of what I said wasn't real but they loved me all the same.

I learned later on that the great Master Ming had been travelling through various villages to choose the students for the next year. He was travelling through our village, talking to the local merchants and villagers.

Master Ming overheard my parents talking about this dream one day when they thought no one was around. He asked them about it and they immediately tried to deny it. They tried to tell him that it was just a dream my father had. He said that he needed to find the person who had that dream. It was very important for him to find this person. There was something very special that he had to give that person.

My parents denied it for a number of days. During these few days they heard about Master Ming from their neighbours and learned that he was searching for his next students. It was then that my parents decided that it would be good to find out what it was that Master Ming had in mind.

When Master Ming said that the person with the dream was chosen to be his student that year, my parents were shocked. They couldn't believe that Master Ming would waste such a precious gift on someone who might be thought of as a witch. They thought that they needed to be honest with Master Ming. Then at least he could give his scholarship to someone worthy of it.

But when they told Master Ming that it was their fourteen year old daughter who dreamed of that special tree and to please give the spot away to another deserving student, his response was not what they expected. Master Ming still wanted her to be his student. They thought he must not have understood what they said but Master Ming would not be deterred. 'Your daughter is to be my student. I have been looking for her for over ten years. If you will not let her study with me, then her spot will be vacant until she comes.'

My parents were again shocked that Master Ming would hold such a hard view. They considered what he said very carefully before agreeing to let me come and be his student. They were probably secretly very pleased that their daughter was thought of by Master Ming as being a special person and they were also probably relieved that they did not have to keep my secrets in their house any longer. They told me of their encounter with Master Ming and that I was to mind his every word and never to speak to him unless he asked me to.

When I arrived at his home and these gardens, I was immediately drawn to this one tree. It stood out from all the others. It alone was shimmering in the sun. The leaves were not leaves but seeds waiting to blow away in the wind. It was the tree from my dream. And it sang to me.

It was so beautiful. When I put my hands on it, I felt like I had found my best friend. It all just felt so natural.

When Master Ming came over to me, I didn't think. I just said what was on my mind. It was like he was a friend too and a friend of this tree. That's how I came here. At first, I didn't know what to expect. But now that it has been a few months, I see now that things are going better. I have found how I can be useful. I have found how I can fit in. I don't have to hide in the house anymore."

Shin was intrigued with this young girl who seemed to have a wise soul. "My choosing doesn't seem nearly as interesting after that," Shin smiled.

"How did Master choose you?" Lan asked.

"I was a student of the Lao Monastery in the north," Shin started. "I had my life planned out. I was

studying to be a monk. One day, Master Ming came to the monastery and spoke to the Rinpoche. The next thing I knew, Master Ming had chosen me to be one of his students. I didn't know why and neither did Rinpoche, but I didn't question it. I was chosen and I would be his student. It was a privilege."

Lan was glad that she was able to talk to Shin. He was a quiet man who kept to himself most of the time. He spent his time working and meditating. She trusted him implicitly now.

Over the next few weeks, the five students started to cut down the trees for the cabin. It had to be a fairly large cabin to hold the five of them and allow room for some cooking. After chopping down several trees, Shin suddenly turned to Lan. "Lan, what about your tree? We can't see which one is your tree. What if we accidentally cut it down?"

Lan had not thought about her tree since she had last talked to Shin about it. She had become so caught up in the practical work at hand and immersed in the task of building the cabin that she did not have time to sing or dream. In fact, she was enjoying the fact that she was not dreaming about the tree anymore. She had found a place for herself where she could live with people and contribute in a meaningful way. When she thought about it now, she did not think of the tree as special or beautiful anymore. Even when she tried to find her tree, she couldn't. If it was there, she couldn't tell it apart from the others.

"It doesn't matter anymore," Lan said. "The important thing is that we are building our cabin and the tree is serving the larger good." Lan felt secretly glad that she saw the tree just like the others did when they first arrived. She saw it as a sign that she was starting to fit in.

"There is the spirit little sister," Lang piped in. "She is growing up."

They continued cutting the trees for the remainder of the week. During these days though, Lan saw Quiang speaking to Lang more often and sometimes it was not so quiet. She overheard snatches of their conversation and knew they were talking about her tree. "It was a special tree," she heard Quiang say. "She has to find it!" She wished that they would stop and just forget about the tree like she had done for several weeks.

"What if we accidentally cut that tree?" Quiang continued. "None of us can see which one it is and it held enough significance that Master Ming made note of it on the first day."

Finally Lang said to Lan, "Why don't you tell us which one is your tree so we can make sure we don't cut it down?"

Lan looked up at him and all of the men, hesitated and then said, "I can't tell anymore. They all look the same. It doesn't matter anyway. I hate that tree. It's better if we cut it down. It will be for a good cause. We need a cabin now. We don't need a 'special tree'."

"There you go Quiang. If little sister can't see it, then none of us can see it. We need to keep working. The cold weather is coming soon."

Quiang looked at Lan in disbelief. "Are you sure you can't see it? Or are you just trying to keep the peace?"

Lan became suddenly angry. "What does it matter? It was just a childish dream! I'm glad I can't see that tree. That tree has caused me nothing but trouble. I have a good thing now. I am working. I belong. I'm contributing. My life is good. Can't you leave it alone?" Lan burst into tears and ran to the lake.

The sad and distraught Lan stayed at the lakeshore for quite some time. After a while, Shin came and sat down beside her. "Why don't they believe me?" she cried to her friend.

"I believe you Lan." Shin held her hand and she leaned her head on his arm. They sat together by the lake as the sun went down.

The five students carried on the next morning forgetting about the outburst that happened the day before. Lan was eager to just get on with the work at hand and nobody questioned her again.

In the middle of one of these days, the noise of the work was interrupted by someone shouting. "STOP! STOP what you're doing!" They all turned around to see Master Ming running toward them.

"Master Ming. Welcome. It is so good to see you. We have been busy living here in the woods. We are just building a cabin for the winter weather. Please join us," Lang greeted him.

Master Ming looked around at the work and the wood being gathered to make the cabin. Impatiently, he said, "You must stop right now! What have you learned? All of you! What have you learned?"

"I've learned how to organize and lead in order to get projects done. I've learned how to make work go efficiently and get more done with less effort. We've learned to work as a team," Lang started.

"I've learned how to support decisions and to draw in the support of others in order to work best together," Tai jumped in.

"And you've done a good job at that," Lang added.

"Master, I have learned that patient consideration and a calm approach is useful in expressing ideas and particularly useful in tempering quick decisions," Quiang said, looking directly at Lang.

Shin said quietly, "I've learned Master that to flow with the moment eases the chaos and tensions of the mind."

"And you Lan? What have you learned?" Master Ming asked Lan.

"Master, I have learned that I can fit in. I have a place in this world and I have contributions that will benefit the larger good. And I don't have dreams anymore. I don't see that special tree anymore and I am happier for it. I have grown up." Lan wasn't sure why she said the last part but she wanted to assert her new found role in this group.

"I see," said Master Ming. "I see that you have made quite a productive little community here. You have learned how to use the resources that Mother Nature has provided and have been very efficient with your efforts.

You are to be congratulated Lang. You have led this group to work as a team and have made bold decisions that people could follow.

Tai, you have been an exemplary support and a practical help in making projects work. Quiang, you are quite right when you say that a clear and considered approach balances all bold moves and you have provided a counterpoint for Lang's quick decisions.

Shin, you have been the quiet voice that listens to Mother Nature and finds your place with her without disturbing her.

Lan, I can see that you have found a place in this group and that you have also found happiness with your new role.

These are all commendable achievements and for that, you are to be congratulated. You have not, however, learned the lesson that I brought you out here to learn. And I came out here as late as I could before you cut off your chances altogether."

All of the students looked at Master Ming and then each other in bewilderment. "Was this another puzzle?" they thought to themselves. "He brought us out here to learn a lesson but he never even told us what we were supposed to learn. And then he has the nerve to tell us we didn't learn it," Lang thought to himself.

"With respect Master, what was the lesson we were supposed to learn?" Lang asked.

Master Ming turned slowly to Shin. "Why don't you tell them Shin?"

Shin closed his eyes and then said, "It was about Lan's tree. It was a special tree. We shouldn't have continued on without knowing where it was. We may have already cut it down."

"But you heard her yourself, Shin. She didn't care about it anymore. And besides, she couldn't even see it anymore," Lang said impatiently.

"That's right Master. I did say that. I wanted them to cut it down," Lan volunteered, more in an effort to support the team than wanting to confront Master Ming.

"I know Lan. That's why I let it go on so long. I knew you were finding your way in a new world you had never experienced before and one that you were enjoying very much. But I came to stop it before it went on too long, too far.

Shin is right. It is about your tree Lan. And even though you can't see it right now, it is still there. It is still shimmering in the sun and the seeds are still ripening, waiting to blow away in the wind, just like you dreamed all those years and just like you saw it when you arrived half a year ago. The only difference is you aren't open to it anymore. Tell me, can you hear it sing anymore?"

"Of course not Master Ming. I haven't heard it sing in months," Lan answered.

"Yes, of course not. It is still standing in the garden. It does still sing. But only I can hear it. And do you know why I can hear it and I can see it?" All the students waited expectantly for his answer.

"Because my heart is open to it. I saw that tree of yours Lan from the time it was a small plant. I nurtured it, watered it and helped it to grow into the tree it is now. It is a special tree not just because it is your tree Lan, but because it is a 'Possibility Tree'. It is a tree of dreams. It connects with your soul and when you can see it, it gives you strength, it gives you power, it gives you life."

"But Master Ming," Lan interrupted, "I didn't feel powerful. It was a curse. It kept me away from life. Other people teased me. I felt awful after a while. I'm glad I don't see things that others don't see anymore."

"Yes I know Lan. But what you've done is no different than what many before you have done. You allowed yourself to forget about a very important part of who you are in order to fit in with a group of people; with a community. And to do that, you had to give up your unique gift, your ability to see that tree, your vision."

"I am humbled by your attention Master Ming, but I did not intend to give it up, it just happened. I moved on to do other things and I don't know if I could have prevented it if I tried.

"That may be true. And perhaps it is also true that the environment and people around you were not conducive to that happening," Master Ming turned to look at Lang and Tai.

Lang looked at Tai briefly before responding. "We meant no harm to Lan Master. We were only teasing her in fun."

"It is not only our intentions but the impact of our actions that we must concern ourselves with, Lang. Many a war has been started when an initially well-intentioned action was received as an insult. When these injuries are not reconciled, they become bruises, open sores or major wounds. And sometimes, healing does not happen until long after much damage is done," Master Ming said calmly.

"Lan, if you had a choice, would you have preferred to experience both your connection to your special tree as well as your sense of belonging and contributing to a group of people?"

Lan was hesitant to reply to this as she felt it would jeopardize her place in the group or somehow anger the students who used to make fun of her. "I don't know Master. I didn't really need that tree," she finally whispered.

Shin spoke up. "Over the last few months, I have noticed some very unusual and beautiful plants in the northern part of the woods Master. They seem quite different than Lan's description of her tree but I feel drawn to them and I've spent my meditation time near them. Are these my 'Possibility Trees?'"

"You never mentioned that you saw these trees too Shin," Lang said.

"I didn't think it was important. I didn't connect it to what we were doing. I saw it as my own personal connection to the universal spirit," Shin replied.

"Do you think that if all of the other students talked about seeing their own Possibility Trees that you might have mentioned it?" Master Ming asked.

"Yes, then I might have mentioned it as a matter of interest but it would not have changed how I perceived them as a personal connection." Shin thought a moment.

"Was there something I should have done to protect Lan's ability to stay connected to her Possibility Tree Master Ming?" Shin asked.

"You should ask Lan that question," Master Ming replied.

Shin looked at Lan. Lan said, "No, there was nothing you could have done."

Master Ming said, "Think Lan. Remember what Shin said."

After another moment, Lan said quietly, "Well, maybe if you told me about your experience of seeing your own tree that might have made a difference."

Shin nodded. He understood. He had spent most of his life meditating and following the rigid routine of the monastery. There was no value placed on sharing his own personal or unique experiences. It was the work of the collective that was important, how each contributed to the welfare of all. His own personal meditation was for the purpose of strengthening his own mind and soul to receive enlightenment and to act with goodness.

Now, for the first time, he saw how his own act of sharing his personal experience was helpful to the collective. He was the light, not for the world, not for society, but for another soul. He realized how one person's personal experience can serve as a light for another soul. And because of this, he also understood that he had the responsibility of being a soul light, a human light. He understood Master Ming's lesson.

"Thank you Master Ming. I understand."

"I know you do Shin."

"But Master," Lang started, "how were we supposed to know this when we were pre-occupied with trying to fend for ourselves? We thought we were meeting the expectations you had for us."

Master Ling answered. "And how does this mirror life outside of this garden Lang? Or perhaps Quiang could answer this."

Quiang pondered his response for a moment. "In the world outside this garden and in the world I have experienced, there are always those who want to lead men to progress. They believe that progress, ingenuity and technical developments are the destiny of men and that this path is to be followed to its ultimate conclusion which is the taming of the earth and the total dominance of man over his environment. This path is alluring and there are many who would support and convince others that this is the best way. I believe that Lang represents this view and he and Tai have convinced us that this is the best way to live.

There are others who believe that moderation and a balance of modern improvements with adherence to the lessons of the earth are needed to live in peace and wisdom and to be true stewards for our children. I believe that Shin and I represent that philosophy. And then there are a very few people in the world who are either shunned and outcast or hailed as a saviour. Those are people gifted with a sight of things yet to be. I believe Lan is one of those people. So, in our small group, we played out what goes on in most of our villages. We agreed that the most important thing was to work towards progress and…"

"But we had to do something to survive!" Lang interrupted. "What would you have us do, just meditate and pray that food was going to cook itself over the fire?"

Lang was incredulous. He had been generous and charitable, helping the group to organize and work together for the common good. Now he felt his efforts being rejected. If this was what he was supposed to learn, maybe this special teaching wasn't for him.

"Let me finish Lang," Quiang continued. "We did work together well and we accomplished great things because of it. And some of us were also able to incorporate our own personal spiritual practices into this routine without sacrificing our ability to contribute to the welfare of the group. But one of us was gifted with special sight. And this was lost. Even though we did our best to try and accommodate this, it was already too late.

Some are able to hold onto their special ability against all conditions and some are not. Most of us see this as a good thing. We say that they have grown up or matured or are more realistic. They can get on with their lives and be a full and contributing citizen in our world.

Lan wanted so much to be one of us and to fit in that she willingly gave up her gift to do this. Even though it wasn't intentional, we all contributed to Lan losing her vision and almost losing her special tree. My guess is that it is not just Lan's tree. It really is our tree…" Quiang stopped here, not knowing how to continue. He had not talked this much in his entire time in Master Ming's garden.

Now, he was telling everyone and Master Ming how he thought the world worked. He must have seemed very arrogant. He felt a little ashamed for allowing himself to go on so long. But Shin continued on where he left off.

"It is our tree because it represents the tree we too have somewhere but haven't yet discovered. It represents the possibility of things not yet here. It represents the hope that we could have but don't. It represents what could be ours if we were open to it. It represents the unknown, the mystery of life. And it is only through

our connection with the earth that we become open."
Shin stopped.

It had been said now. This was the totality of their lesson. Shin and Quiang were silent, looking down at the ground. This was a lesson that had been growing in their hearts from the beginning but they were not accustomed to speaking so boldly.

Quiang had lived his life supporting the visions of other men in his village. His family was not powerful and he watched his father yield to others. He had taught Quiang the art of diplomacy and submission in all of his dealings even when he knew he was right. Quiang had tried to talk quietly to Lang about his thoughts but it did not come out as clearly as it did just now in front of Master Ming. Even now, Quiang felt uneasy about speaking so openly.

Master Ming stood silently, watching the five students' faces as they took in this long explanation of his lesson. He was not convinced that all of his students understood the depth of its wisdom. In fact, it was the only lesson he would teach them during their entire time with him.

Quiang and Shin, he could see, did understand the full purpose of this exercise. Their lesson would be to bring the full purpose of this exercise to life in the vibrancy of the world outside. They now needed to voice their beliefs and to share their wisdom in a way that would change the course of society. They had to live their beliefs and create action in the world. Their actions had to make a difference. They could no longer simply lock themselves in a monastery or submit to others' beliefs. Their ideas also needed to be heard and seen in their actions.

Lang and Tai, Master Ming could also see, were only half convinced of these ideas. Although they were trying their best to get the most out of the opportunity to learn with Master Ming they were already fully immersed in the ways of the world, the ways of men and in the ways of worldly progress. They were trying to grasp the significance of the words that Quiang spoke, but clearly, they did not fully understand. Lang and Tai represented the majority of those in the world outside.

"Thank you for your words Quiang and Shin. I know you believe in what you say. However, as Lang put it, 'What does this have to do with getting fed and simply surviving?' You have experienced one way of living life and in many ways, it works marvellously. Your next lesson is to take what you have learned today and live your life accordingly. I will see you in another month."

Master Ming turned up the path he came from without a word and disappeared from sight. The students stood silently and watched him leave, dumbfounded at how their encounter with their teacher along with the day, ended so abruptly.

Turning to the rest of the group, Lang spoke first. "Well, I guess that's that. Master Ming has spoken and so have Quiang and Shin. I guess Tai and I are clearly outnumbered and will need to accept that with humility."

It wasn't clear if he was humbled by the experience, or if he really accepted the fact that he and Tai were outnumbered. Lang's words hung in the air.

"We should figure out what we should do. There is still the matter of surviving in the cold weather for the next month," Tai offered. "We still need to consider the reality of that."

"Perhaps Lan could enlighten us all about how we should proceed then," Lang said with a slightly sarcastic edge.

"Stop it!" Lan yelled. "It's not my fault! I did everything I was supposed to. I helped out with everything and I worked hard too! It's not my fault that Master Ming favours this tree. I wish I never saw it. I wish I never came here! I wish I were dead!" Lan ran from the group crying.

Shin started to move to follow her. Lang stopped him. "Let her cry for a while. It will give us some time to think about what we should do." Shin sat back down.

"Tree or no tree, we still need to stay warm and eat during this month. Since you and Quiang seem to know more about the other-worldly aspects of living, why don't you come up with a plan for how we are supposed to deal with that? Tai and I will continue building our shelter. Do you agree?" He looked at Quiang and Shin. Since neither of them had any better plan for the time being, they nodded. By nightfall, the group had collected their thoughts and things had settled down.

Meanwhile, as light was fading in his garden, Master Ming sat under a tree looking west. The sun sank like it was dripping down the mountain. He closed his eyes and listened. He started to hum and then stopped. Silently, he opened his eyes, got up and walked back to the house.

Lan ran as hard as her legs could take her. She didn't stop until she knew she was far away from the group. But the crying didn't stop for a long time. She couldn't remember a time when she felt this confused, angry, resentful and desperate all at the same time. Even when her parents kept her isolated in their house, she never felt this distraught. It was like she was torn between the person she was and the person she was becoming. It hurt even more to be told that it wasn't right to become this person who was happier and more productive. It stung to be told she had to stay the way she was and couldn't grow up.

Everyone else got to grow up. Why couldn't she? And why were these grown up's, these elders trying to tell her about her own life and who she was? After all, it was her life. It was supposed to be up to her to say who she was and what was important.

She could just leave. There was nothing keeping her here. She wasn't a prisoner after all. No one was forcing her to be Master Ming's student. But she knew

in her heart that this was not the time to abandon all
that she had come for. Her parents were so proud to be
parents of a student of Master Ming. It was an honour
to be chosen as a student. And Master Ming held a
special place for her specifically. She wasn't sure yet but
there was something he had in mind for her. That much
she knew.

She didn't have the heart to disappoint her parents
nor give up the opportunity given to her by Master Ming.
She just didn't know what he expected of her. Why didn't
he just tell her what she should do? And if that tree
was so special, why didn't he just tell everyone from the
beginning that they should respect this fact? Why leave
it up to chance whether she went the right way or not?

She just did not understand his methods. It left her
feeling alone and at odds with her world, not unlike the

way she often felt at home. She did not like this feeling, but there didn't seem to be any solution to her dilemma and she fell asleep with all of her mixed emotions churning inside her.

When morning came, Lan awoke to the sound of birds she had not heard before. They were melodious songs coming from what seemed like tiny little birds all around her. She opened her eyes and saw colourful birds flying around from tree to tree, singing to all the others doing the same thing.

She looked around. In this small meadow was a clearing she had not seen before. The gentle slope came down to a lake. Around the grass were woods with small trees. The trees were just the right size for her to be able to break thin branches and start a fire. She had watched the men start fires over the last several months and even

though she had not had much opportunity to start them herself, she remembered the technique.

There were berries in nearby bushes that could be picked and eaten and there were even some fruit trees farther in the clearing. She saw plenty of little squirrels and rabbits in the clearing. Lan was confident that, given some time and practice, she could probably catch some of them herself. She pondered this new, wondrous place. It was as though Master Ming created this garden just for her to learn how to survive with Mother Nature.

For two weeks, Lan was able to sustain herself with berries and fruit. But she soon realized that she would need to do more than that once the colder weather came. Her fires needed to last longer. She would need to cut down more branches, maybe even whole trees to keep herself warm. She needed to build a more permanent shelter and obtain warmer clothing. These were things that she had not considered.

Now she wished that she were again with the other students. They would know what to do. They at least could help each other survive. But for some reason, Lan could not bring herself to join them again. Her sense of newly found independence and freedom was liberating and she wanted to enjoy its rewards for a little while longer.

For two more weeks, Lan spent time alone, walking around the clearing, exploring other parts of the garden area she chose to call her own. She spent time meditating, an activity that Shin taught her, and singing. She felt as though she was beginning to connect with herself again and to listen and respond to the earth like she used to.

It was in this state that she decided to rejoin the group of students. She felt as though she could fit in and contribute something valuable, not only because of what she had learned about living in the wild, but because she knew something of who she was and what she had to offer.

The first person to greet her was Shin, the person she most wanted to see again. He was pleased to see her. He dropped what he was doing and gave her a hug. He called out to the others who were nearby and the other three students appeared almost immediately. Shouts of excitement sprang from their lips as they recognized her.

Lang exclaimed loudly. "What a great day to have our little sister back! We should celebrate today." The three others agreed wholeheartedly and they whisked her away to ask about her month and to tell her about theirs.

Lan was surprised to see how genuinely they all seemed to care about her wellbeing. When she talked about how it took a while to get acquainted with the environment around her, she saw four heads nodding in empathy.

Lang was the first to speak and he seemed quite humbled by the quick words of Master Ming a month ago. "I didn't realize how worldly I was. I only saw myself as ultimately practical and productive. I was a leader. I knew that from my dealings in the world. And when all of you followed my lead, it was natural to try to do my best for all of us. I was truly shocked when Master Ming reacted so sharply. It made me take account of my intentions.

This last month has been an eye-opener for me. Not only did I not acknowledge the unique gifts or contributions that you each brought but I judged the contributions that you did share with our community only according to its instrumental value, how it would build the community, how to make progress. It has been very hard but I have been learning about reflection and meditation from Shin and about thoughtful action from Quiang. Shin has been a very kind and generous teacher. But here I am talking again. Shin, you should have stopped me."

Shin looked grateful for the acknowledgement of his contribution and the praise from Lang, but he did not allow this to go straight to his ego. He spoke eloquently and succinctly. "Lang has demonstrated how vast the human spirit is and how we are amenable to change and wisdom. But I do not want to exclude Quiang and Tai for they have each taught all of us something of the world and of the earth in this last month. Please share with us what you have discovered."

Lan could not believe how almost wary they each were of dominating the group. Each one in turn shared a little of their learning and experience and each one of them showed sincere gratitude for the lesson that Master Ming had taught them one month ago.

Tai went on to describe the study he had made of some of the birds and wildlife in the area and the plants that he had come across, touching on their properties and potential medicinal benefits. He had never allowed himself the time to pursue this interest of his before but he had become fascinated with the garden.

Lan became suddenly aware that this was a side of Tai that she had never seen and that it changed her perspective of him. She was very interested in what he had to say. Tai could see that she was very attentive to every detail he shared. "I would be happy to share my drawings and discoveries with you in more detail." Lan was delighted at the offer and accepted with enthusiasm.

Lang then introduced Quiang's great gift for words and theatre. "I never knew the joys and the challenge of drama. I was always very focused on the practical aspects of life, of progress and of efficiency. Quiang has taught us…me at least…to stop and think about how our actions affect each other and our world. I have never laughed so much in my life. And I have never wondered so much about my own impact on the world around me. So, for little sister, I would like to ask Quiang to share his great drama called 'Life in the Garden'."

And with that, Quiang sprang to his feet like a deer taking flight. He changed from a quiet contemplative person to one who was full of intensity, and then someone confused, then another change again. He was displaying the whole experience of their life in Master Ming's garden in a condensed, amusing and thought provoking way. This was something that Lan had never experienced before. She could see things so clearly through Quiang's clever mixture of words, expressions and actions. Yes, this was exactly what had happened to them all. The lessons, the burdens and the confusions. When he was finished, all the students stood up cheering and clapping. Quiang, obviously pleased to have delighted his audience, gave a large smile and laugh as he bowed numerous times to each of them.

"So you see little sister," Lang continued, "much has developed since you last saw us. We have each taken the time to discover a little more of who we are. We have taken the time to pursue our interests and talents. We have shared ourselves with each other and we have come to appreciate the gifts that each of us brings to our little community.

I have learned so much about myself as well. Of course, it is my natural inclination to want to lead and speak. And I definitely have a preference for worldly things and the workings of our society but I have tempered that. I have realized that if my way were the only right path, then Master Ming would have celebrated our accomplishments those many months ago rather than chastise us.

Our community is enriched with the perspectives and gifts that each of us brings, even if I did not see them as valuable before. I never would have thought that the artist was an essential aspect of our society. Now, I can see how out of balance I could have led us to become without the biting insight of his words. He is a mirror for us to see ourselves. And if I may continue with that analogy, Tai has become our magnifying glass to inspect and learn about the world around us and Shin has been a prism into our soul; that we may grow spiritually."

"And Lang has been a lantern to see the way ahead," Shin added.

"Yes, and if he trips and falls, I as the mirror show him how he looks on the ground," Quiang said quickly.

"And Tai here inspects all of his cuts and bruises!" They all laughed as Lang blushed.

After a moment, Lang joined in as well. "Well I guess humility has never been my favourite personality trait," he chuckled.

"But we have not heard yet from you, little sister. Tell us about your months in the garden."

At that, all the men stopped laughing and turned to listen to Lan. At first, she hesitated as she had not thought about putting her experience into words, but as she started, she could not seem to get all the words out of her mouth fast enough.

Lan described her anger and her confusion about Master Ming's visit. She described her childhood, her

before Master Ming's last lesson. She didn't know what she was doing or how she was going to survive. She just wanted to run away from everything and everyone. As she said these words, Lan cried.

It was the first time she had confided all of her feelings about her life to anyone, much less a group of people. But she could hardly control herself. It was as though the words came out on their own accord and the feelings along with them. When she looked up at the other students, she could see some tears on their faces as well. And rather than a look of disdain or contempt, she saw understanding and compassion, as though they had experienced similar feelings in their own lives.

With the group's encouragement, she then shared how she found a clearing that seemed to have popped out of nowhere, as though it was created exactly for her at that moment. It seemed to say to her, "Stay here for a while. No one will hurt you here." It was where she stayed for the rest of her time before coming back. She found everything she needed there.

As time went by, she learned how to keep herself warm, how to gather berries and even hunt for small animals and cook them. She was surprised at her own resilience and independence and proud of the fact that she could do these things. She found herself feeling more connected with the earth and finally, with herself. It was only then that she dared to think about returning. "I found out who I am," she said. And without even thinking, she said, "I am a healer."

When Lan said those last words 'I am a healer' she thought to herself, "Where did that come from? I didn't know that before." But when she spoke the words, she knew that they were true. She felt a peace within herself. Yes, I am a healer.

And even more surprising to Lan, the other students didn't even seem as shocked at this revelation as she was. Their faces said, "Ah, yes. Of course."

As she was contemplating these things, Shin said, "There is something else that we want to show you." The students nodded to each other and Shin motioned to her to follow him. He led her down a wooded path and the other three students followed.

"What is it?" Lan asked.

"You'll see," Shin said. After a few minutes, they came upon a clearing and before them stood the most glorious tree with shimmering leaves that she had ever seen.

"My tree," Lan whispered. The tears flowed down her cheeks as she walked up to the tree. It was larger than she remembered and certainly more beautiful. But it was definitely her tree. She felt it. She knew it. She put her hands on the tree and closed her eyes. She was feeling her own heartbeat. She was home.

Time seemed to be endless and when she was ready to take her hands off the tree and open her eyes, the students were all still there as though only a moment had passed.

"How did you find it? I thought you couldn't see it?" Lan asked.

Lang answered this time. "As we came to know ourselves more, each one of us in turn discovered a very beautiful tree in the garden. When I found it, I thought at first it was yours as yours was the only tree that was ever described as shimmering. But when I got closer, I saw that it was not yours. Or I should say, I felt it. It was as though the tree was calling my name. I knew it was not your tree but my own. It was a very unusual feeling. I had never had feelings like it before. Something was calling within me and from the tree at the very same time.

It took me awhile to tell the others about the tree, but when I did, I found that each of them had had a very similar experience."

"My tree was not a tree at all but more like a flowering bush," Tai said. "It was the most beautiful thing I had ever seen. And it kept changing every time I looked at it. It was endlessly enchanting."

"My tree was not a tree at all but a vine," Shin said, "Some who do not see it would say that it is like a weed that grows everywhere but can you imagine having lights

that are strung around the entire garden? That is like my tree. My string of lights," Shin said.

"But how could you see my tree? I thought I would be the only one who could see it." Lan asked.

"That is the most interesting thing," Lang added excitedly. "As we came to know each other more and to appreciate each other more fully, we could also see one another's trees. And we could sense whose tree it was. When we finally shared our experiences, that sense became stronger. It was only natural that we came to see your tree. We had gotten to know you and as our knowledge of you grew, your tree stood out clearly."

Lang stopped, looked at the others and looked down on the ground before continuing. "It was a good thing that Master Ming came out when he did. You remember that your tree was not in a clearing but was in amongst tall grass and other trees?" Lan nodded. "Well, we had cut down the area to gather wood and your tree would have been the next tree we would have cut. Master Ming stopped us just in time."

Lan gasped. Her mind raced with the possibilities that would have come from that. Would she have discovered herself? Would she have lost herself forever? Would there have been the possibility that she would never have known she was a healer?

"I know what you're thinking." Lang seemed to read her mind. "We have asked ourselves as well what the consequence of that action would have been. But Shin and Tai have reminded us that Mother Earth has wisdom beyond us. Mother Earth does heal. New life does grow even after being cut down. Your Possibility Tree would have grown back, but it might have taken a long time. It might have taken your whole life for the tree to blossom as it does now.

Lan's mind was still reeling. "I think it may take me a while to catch up with you all. I hope you will allow me to get to know each of you as well as you already know each other." "Of course, little sister," Quiang laughed. "We have as much time as Master Ming allows us to have in his garden."

Over the next few weeks, Lan got to know each of the students more fully and more deeply. She was amazed that she did not see the beauty in each of them in their first months together. Now, it seemed as though each of them was so perfect and yet so different that they were more than human.

At first, she was shy to admit that she could not see each of their trees but within a few weeks they were all shimmering and glowing. How could she not see such obvious beauty before? In just a short time, she became introduced to Tai's knowledge of plants, which she in turn, instinctively knew how to use for the ailments that came her way.

Quiang's poetry and dramas kept her mind and heart wondering about the human spirit and all the possibilities for good and evil that dwelt within it. Shin's quiet teaching kept her in touch with herself and with Mother Earth which she treasured beyond measure.

And Lang. Beyond his convivial and naturally charismatic personality was a gentle and compassionate man, capable of great things beyond the material world. His was the last tree to become visible to her and when it did, she knew something even more. It was the tree just beyond her own. And if hers was the next to be cut down, his would have followed. He did not even know himself at that time. They were stopped before the whole community's heart and soul were destroyed. In her heart, Lan quietly thanked Master Ming for his wisdom.

It was just a few days after this that they heard the news. One of the servants came down to the garden. Lang went up to speak to him. When he came back, his face was long.

"Master Ming has died."

Lan's heart sank. She was just beginning to know who she was and to appreciate the others. There was so much more that she had to learn, that she had hoped Master Ming could teach her, teach all of them. It was too soon for him to die. The lessons were unfinished. She wasn't finished. She wasn't ready to hear this news. "Couldn't anybody help him?" Lan said with desperation.

"Apparently Master Ming knew that he was dying even before he took us on as students. He instructed his servants not to mention a word about it to us. That was why he did not spend much time with us. He was very weak much of the time but did not want to give us any indication. He had prepared our lessons beforehand and had written down his final words and wishes to be read upon his death. His servants have called for us to be present when these are read tomorrow evening at the house."

Everyone was stunned at the news. No one spoke. All eyes were downcast and each student contemplated what this meant both for themselves and their community. All they learned had come to this. "Let us prepare to attend tomorrow evening. We can show the utmost respect to Master's teachings by exemplifying what we have learned here in the garden. There is nothing more that Master would have wanted us to do," Lang said quietly.

They each turned to console the next student. Tears and words of comfort were exchanged. A solemn day passed.

The students arrived to a house already full with people paying respects. He had died a full week before the servants told the students so arrangements and communication had already gone out quickly to people far away and many travelled miles to attend.

The students had not stopped to think about what a large gathering this would be but upon reflection, it was to be expected that someone of such high regard would have many dignitaries and former students attending such an occasion.

Ming Zhou Cho

Although the remembrance could have been very grand considering the people in attendance, there was no such pomp and circumstance. The words and prayers were plain and simple yet full of significance and deep sentiment.

One of Master Ming's closest servants came forward to speak. "On behalf of all of us at the house, I thank you all for attending and paying respects to our most revered and respected teacher, Master Ming. Master knew that he was dying and had carefully prepared words to be spoken on this occasion. I will read this on his behalf as he wished."

*To my dear friends, students, colleagues*

*I am speaking to you now as spirit. I have passed into the ethereal world and live now* only in your hearts and thoughts. I know that you have each brought richness and a depth to this world for I have heard of your endeavours through the years. I thank you all for allowing me to help you bring peace and love to your hearts.

I would like to speak to you all now of the legacy of my teaching. Of course this legacy is only possible with the willingness and openness of all of you.

My loyal servants: my wish is that you and your families continue to be stewards of the house and that this house may be a warm welcome to any who come to visit.

My students Lang, Tai, Quiang, Shin and Lan: You were my final students and I chose you with purpose and intent. I chose you to be stewards of the garden. As you know by now, the garden is very special. By the time you hear these words, I know you have each found your tree and can see the magical trees of the others. You may have guessed by now that I not only cared for Lan's tree but each of your trees until you came this year. The garden is full of these trees, these Possibility Trees. Each one of the people in attendance can show you their tree in the garden and as you come to know them, you will see them shine and shimmer.

*Lang, Tai, Quiang, Shin and Lan, you
are the keepers of the Possibility Trees. You
have learned in this short time the wisdom
to connect with Mother Earth, the stillness
to discover yourselves and the humility to
appreciate the gifts of others. My Possibility
Tree has now died along with my body, but
the seeds of that tree are now planted in you.
You and Mother Earth are now the keepers of
trees. Now I rest.*

*Ming Zhou Cho*

There was a silence of reverence in the room.
Everyone was absorbing these final words from the
Master. None were more surprised than the five students
about what this document contained. They were still

adjusting to the fact that Master Ming was no longer with them. To be left as stewards of the garden seemed ludicrous and daunting. And yet, after everyone had paid their last respects to Master Ming and saw him received into the garden and kind and gentle Mother Earth, most people came to speak to the students.

"I will help you as much as I can. Master Ming changed my heart about adversity, enemies and seeking revenge. Please come to me with any questions you may have."

"Thank you for tending the garden. You must be very special to have been chosen by Master Ming."

"This will not be an easy path. I will help with any burdens I can."

They each offered support and practical help. The servants also offered to help the new masters with their work.

"The new masters?" Lan thought. "This is a mistake. I am not a master. I am a girl."

Lang spoke as though he could hear her thoughts. "We can do this together, all of us. We each bring something to our community, to our world. We each bring something to each other. You heard Master Ming yourselves: 'the wisdom to connect with Mother Earth, the stillness to discover yourselves and the humility to appreciate the gifts of others'. This is what Master Ming was helping us to learn. And this is what we have to teach others."

Lang always had much more confidence, Lan thought. The other students seemed willing but she was still unsure.

Lang continued. "We each bring something unique to our community. Tai is curious about how the world works, every aspect of it. I have a sense of how people can work together, to lead. Shin brings us inside ourselves and our own growth. Quiang reminds us that our lives have some meaning and aesthetic beyond practicality. And Lan connects us with Mother Earth and is a healer. We need each one of us to be able to show the wholeness of Master Ming's teachings. With one of us gone, it will be unbalanced, only the partial meaning will be conveyed. Will you each join me in continuing Master's legacy? Will you be keepers of the trees?"

Keepers of the trees. Stewards of the garden. A girl becoming a woman. Students becoming masters. As Lang continued, Lan walked alone to her tree. She sat next to the tree, put her hands on the trunk and closed her eyes. Softly she started singing the songs that she sang when she first arrived. As the last song ended, she opened her eyes and her heart opened inside her. She smiled. "Yes," she said out loud. "I am home."

CPSIA information can be obtained
at www.ICGtesting.com
Printed in the USA
LVIW02n0609300913
354492LV00001B

9 781460 200827